Little Red Riding Hood

and the Big Bad Wolf!

For Abbie, Leo, and Harry

Text copyright © 2015 by Nosy Crow
Illustrations copyright © 2013 by Nosy Crow
Nosy Crow and its logos are trademarks of Nosy Crow Ltd. Used under license.

First U.S. edition 2017

Library of Congress Catalog Card Number pending
ISBN 978-0-7636-9331-2

17 18 19 20 21 22 GBL 10 9 8 7 6 5 4 3 2 1

Printed in Shenzhen, Guangdong, China

This book was typeset in Clarendon.
The illustrations were created digitally.

Nosy Crow
an imprint of
Candlewick Press
99 Dover Street
Somerville, Massachusetts 02144

www.nosycrow.com
www.candlewick.com

Little Red Riding Hood

illustrated by
Ed Bryan

An imprint of Candlewick Press

Once upon a time, there was
a kind and helpful girl named
Little Red Riding Hood.
She lived with her mother in a
cottage at the edge of a forest.

One morning, Little Red Riding Hood's mother said, "Oh, Little Red Riding Hood, your **grandmother** isn't feeling well. Would you please take her **a basket of food?**"

Soon the basket was packed
and Little Red Riding Hood
was ready to go.

As Little Red Riding Hood was leaving,
her mother gave her a warning.
"Be **careful** in the forest and beware
of the **Big Bad Wolf!**" she said.

And Little Red Riding Hood went on her way.

She had not gone very far before the **Big Bad Wolf** appeared.

"Hello, little girl," said the wolf. "Where are you going?"
"Oh, just to my grandmother's with this basket of food,"
said Little Red Riding Hood, and off she went.

Little Red Riding Hood soon came to a clearing in the forest filled with **flowers.**
"How **pretty!**" said Little Red Riding Hood.

She knew that her grandmother **loved daisies**, so she picked some and put them in her basket. Then she continued on her way.

Little Red Riding Hood skipped through the forest until she came to a big **oak tree.**

"Oh, look!" she said.
"What lovely **acorns**!
I'll put some in my basket.
You never know when they
might come in handy."

With the **flowers** and the **acorns**
in her basket, Little Red Riding Hood
continued on her way.

Little Red Riding Hood wandered along, and, by and by, she came across a **bear** with a **huge** pot of **honey**.

"Hello," said the bear.
"Can you help me pour this **honey** into my jars? You can take a jar with you if you do."
So Little Red Riding Hood stopped to help the bear.

Then, with the **flowers**, the **acorns**, and the **honey** in her basket, Little Red Riding Hood skipped off through the trees.

Finally, Little Red Riding Hood arrived at her grandmother's house.

"Hello, Grandma!" she called. "I'm here with a basket **full** of nice things!"
"I'm in bed, my dear," called a voice through the door.

It was quite **dark** inside the cottage, but
Little Red Riding Hood thought her
grandmother looked a bit different.

"Oh, Grandma, what **big ears** you have!"
said Little Red Riding Hood.

"All the better to
hear you with,
my dear . . ." came
the reply.

"Oh, Grandma, what **big eyes** you have!"
said Little Red Riding Hood.

"All the better to **see** you
with, my dear . . ."
came the reply.

"Oh, Grandma, what **big teeth** you have!"
said Little Red Riding Hood.

"**All the better to . . .**

eat you with, my dear!"
said the Big Bad Wolf.
He had been disguised
as Grandma all along!

And with that, the wolf **jumped** out of the bed and **chased** Little Red Riding Hood around the room!

Quickly, Little Red Riding Hood **reached** into her basket. She took out the **flowers** and waved them under the wolf's **nose.**

The wolf **sneezed**
and **sneezed**
and **sneezed!**

But **that** didn't
stop him for long.

So Little Red Riding Hood **reached** into her basket **again**. She pulled out the **acorns** and threw them on the **floor**.

The wolf skidded
and **slipped**
and **skated**
all over.

But **that** didn't
stop him, either.

So Little Red Riding Hood **reached** into her basket for the **last** time. She took out the jar of **honey** and threw it **all over** the Big Bad Wolf.

"Yuck! I'm covered in **sticky honey!"**
yelped the wolf.

"Just you wait and see
what happens **next!"**
said Little Red
Riding Hood. . . .

The sticky honey smelled **so** delicious that a swarm of **bees** flew in through the window and **chased** the wolf out the door.

The Big Bad Wolf ran down the road and was never, **ever** seen again.

As soon as the Big Bad Wolf was gone,
Little Red Riding Hood unlocked
the cupboard . . .

and out **jumped** Grandma!

LITTLE Red Riding Hood laid out the
delicious food from her basket, then she
and her grandmother had a wonderful feast.
And they both lived **happily** ever after.